THE GOLDEN JOURNEY OF MR. PARADYNE BY WILLIAM J. LOCKE

Jogging southward
on an irrevocable
way, never, in this
life to retrace
his steps.

N
W
E
S

THE GOLDEN JOURNEY OF MR. PARADYNE

MR. COSMO PARADYNE, K.C., awoke. He awoke to an intense consciousness of being wide awake. It was dark. He damned his ill-luck, for he knew that insomnia had marked him for its own for the rest of the night. 'Phillibert v. Phillibert, Cohen & Smith,' would dance through his head till morning. He threw himself into an impatient turn and all but fell out of bed. Indeed, one foot touched the floor. He swung towards the other side and immediately came into contact with a wooden wall.

He lay on his back for some time, his hands over his eyes, wondering. Then he laughed to himself. Why, of course, he was in a ship's bunk. How silly not to realize it at once. It was the Whitsuntide recess, and he and his wife were going on a much needed holiday. He turned over again and composed himself to sleep. But the important will case of 'Phillibert v. Phillibert, Cohen & Smith' worried him.

He should have made application to the Judge in the

Chancery Court before starting on his journey. For the life of him he couldn't remember to have done so. To his client the point was of vast importance.

He racked his brains. On Saturday there had been the consultation at his Chambers with Miss Phillibert and Griffiths, her solicitor. It was arranged that he should make the application on Monday.

That was yesterday.

It was the oddest thing in the world. Even if he himself had forgotten the appointment-a most improbable thing his clerk would have reminded him; his clerk, Gregson, a pallid, clock-faced man, as infallible and implacable as a machine. He shrugged his shoulders. He must have appeared in court and forgotten it. It was high time for him to take a rest. He had been working at high pressure for months, and was dead tired; fagged out.... That old fool of a Phillibert was certainly under undue influence when he made the will. The letter of Mrs. Cohen.... He tossed impatiently. He would dismiss the case from his mind. The only value of a holiday was to clean out your brain and give it a rest. He made mighty resolve to sleep. The blanket slipped and he found himself a-cold. He cursed the hardness and discomfort of ships' bunks as he groped for it on the floor.

It was a very curious ship. There was no creak of the woodwork, no throb of the engines, no motion. The silence of death was only broken by a queer, rhythmical scrunching sound, which seemed like the lap of idle waves against the vessel's side. Either the engines had broken down or the ship was becalmed or befogged.... He snuggled up in the retrieved blanket, all the bedclothes that the ship afforded, and resigned himself to circumstances. After all, it was rest that mattered. Golf was but a means of attaining rest, and Le Touquet....

Le Touquet!

The thought hit him like a hammer. What on earth was he doing on board ship, at dead of night, on his way to Le Touquet which was a cab-drive from Boulogne? He swung out of bed and, standing up, realized for the first time that his legs were bare. His hands plucking at his only garment proved it to be a flannel shirt open at the neck. Never had the unadventurous Paradyne gone to bed in a flannel shirt. For night attire a suit of plate-armour would have been as customary. A bit of the truth flashed upon him. He was not on board ship at all. But where the devil was he? a crowing cock tore the stillness and told him that he was on dry land.

Where the devil was he? In a train? He fumbled round about the bunk for an electric switch and found nothing to correspond with a sleeping-car's accessories. His bare feet trod bare and gritty boards. a swept-out hand hit-so that his knuckles were grazed-something cold and hard, which in its turn rattled loud against a similar substance. He stood still and sweated.

Presently, his eyes accustomed to the darkness, he recognized on the ground a yard-long slit of pale light by the bunk head. That meant a doorway at any rate. He fumbled till he found a key in a lock, thrust the opened door outwards, and stood on the threshold amazed, gazing out into a strange world in the dimmest light of dawn.

There was a road which the near distance swallowed up into nothingness. Vague trees loomed like sentinels. Immediately below three wooden steps at his feet swept a broad stretch of grass bordering the road. Far away across an infinite vastness of plain shimmered the dull lemon and green reflection of some radiance. The rhythmical scrunching sound went on. It was somewhere behind him.

He descended the three steps, recognized that what he had taken for a ship was but a sort of gipsy caravan, and that the noise was made by a tethered horse comfortably munching the wayside grass.

* * * * *

THE most bewildered of young and brilliant leaders of the Chancery Bar, clad only in a flannel shirt reaching to his knees, a vesture of humility for any man counting as religion the decencies of life, returned to the caravan steps and in the dusk of the growing twilight made out that which was therein. Pots and pans and brooms and brushes hanging from roof and walls in a nightmare medley. The bunk was but a thinly cushioned plank, the blanket some dark horror. He entered and his feet grew entangled in what, stooping down, he found to be articles of raiment. He groped and gradually collected a pair of cotton socks, canvas trousers, curiously unfamiliar; yet, on the other hand, his familiar golfing shoes and Norfolk jacket. He dressed himself gladly, for he shivered in the cold of the dawn.

Both phenomena, the cold and the dawn, he realized. Blanket around him, he sat on the threshold of the absurd structure in which, without question, he had his immediate being, clasped his head in his hands and concentrated his mind on the solution of the amazing problem:

'Where am I? And what the devil am I doing here, wherever I am?'

Loss of memory? No. Absurd! He was Cosmo Paradyne, K.C., aged forty-two. All his past life lay an open book to him. Winchester; King's College, Cambridge; the Bar. From childhood an honourable history of ambition, work and success. He was certainly not wandering about like a fool not knowing who he was.

Yet his present circumstances needed elucidation.

Let him trace back things to Friday-or rather start with Friday, the day of Viola's wedding. Viola was his daughter, a very young and modern girl who had made socially, though not financially, an excellent marriage. As Earls and Judges and Cabinet Ministers and their wives could not be expected to turn up at Ealing, where he dwelt, the wedding reception was held at the Hyde Park Hotel. There were two or three hundred people, a band and champagne and wedding presents and detectives and photographers and journalists and a young bridegroom with an Honourable before his name; everything that girlish bride could desire. a great success.

When Cosmo Paradyne came to say good-bye to his daughter, it occurred to him that he was but distantly acquainted with her. Still, he performed his paternal duty.'My dear,' he said, 'I wish you weren't going out to

India, it's so very far away.'

Whereat she laughed. 'You never supposed I was going to live in Ealing all my life.'

He shrugged his shoulders. After all, it mattered very little where one lived.

He remembered the shrug an the reflection. Everything was perfectly clear. His wife drove home in the car. He took a cab to his chambers where some work awaited him, papers to read in connection with that infernal 'Phillibert v. Phillibert, Cohen & Smith.' He took the train to Ealing, dressed, dined alone with Martha. The dinner was not particularly good. He was the last man in the world to insist on delicate cookery. He had neither the time nor the thought for pleasures of the table. But tough mutton was tough mutton; bad for the digestion and therefore bad for work.

His wife, in her thin-lipped, acid, final voice, replied to his remonstrance:

'I think it's exceedingly good mutton. Roach is the best butcher in the neighbourhood. If he weren't, I shouldn't go to him.'

He did not press the point, having given up argument with Martha this many a year. He resumed their disconnected talk about the wedding and mentioned Viola's scornful repudiation of Ealing.

'Perhaps it's a bit suburban,' he said, with a smile.

'It's where I shall end my days,' replied Martha. 'And where, if Viola hadn't married, she would have ended hers.'

She looked, with the pride of possession, around the decorous dining-room, its walls deadly with gloomy oil paintings; two full-length of her father and mother, ugly and awe-inspiring personages. For it was her own house, bequeathed to her (together with other worldly goods) by her father, a prosperous solicitor who had given Cosmo his first brief; and into it had she entered as a bride; and in it had she constructed and developed her own virtuous, dutiful and rigid life.

'You're not getting dissatisfied and wanting to change, I hope?'

'Oh, no, no,' he replied hastily. 'It's good for me to live out of town.'

'You get your fresh air and your golf. ' 'I do,' said he.

He remembered that when the butler came round with a cheese souffle he waved it away.

'I assure you there's nothing wrong with that,' said his wife.

He passed his hand over his lined, clean-shaven face and apologized courteously. During all the twenty years of his married life he had never quarrelled with Martha. He regarded her as a cosmic condition of his existence, like breakfast, rain and fog, and, again like these phenomena, remote from his vital interests. He had no appetite, he said; was too tired to eat; dog-weary; she must forgive him.

'Of course I do,' she replied politely. 'But, all the same, it isn't funny looking after a dead man.'

He was a dry, pragmatic fellow, accustomed to interpret the exact signification of words.

'What do you mean by that?'

'Nothing more than what I said, Cosmo.'

Sitting on the steps of the caravan, he repeated, as these incidents passed through his mind:

'Yes, what the devil did she mean by that?'

He continued his review.

* * * * *

THE dull meal over, he lit his after-dinner cigar, his one concession to the hedonistic, and smoked it as usual, in solitude. Mrs. Paradyne allowed cigarettes, on necessary occasions, in her drawing-room, but never cigars. As it tasted bitter, he threw it away half-smoked and joined his wife, whom he found casting up wedding accounts at her escritoire. After a short while, he bade her good night, kissed a half-turned cheek and, according to unvarying custom when at home, went into his study to work. He was in the middle of a book, *The Relations of Equity to Common Law*, which, luminously written, would supply a long-felt want. He sat down and opened out his manuscript.

* * * * *

THERE his memory failed. What had happened after that? Instinctively he searched his right-hand pocket for his pipe. He found it; but he found something else, too, which caused him mighty astonishment. It was a very short, though somewhat elaborate, silver flageolet.

The dim light of dawn had now overspread the earth so that objects near and far were visible; but, for the next few moments, all that he saw was the bright and alluring instrument in his hands.

Now, Cosmo Paradyne was a musician in a dry and scientific way; furthermore, an authority on the history and use of wind instruments. He had founded the Ealing Symphonic Society and once a month or so played oboe or clarinet at their concerts. He had a fair collection in his study. But this silver flageolet had never been in his possession. He had never seen one like it.

He stared at it, put it to his lips, and, fingering the stops and keys, began to play, without premeditated act of volition, an extraordinary air. But after a few phrases he leaped to his feet in a shiver of fright, dropping the flageolet on the grass. How had this Puckish melody come into his head?

Then, returning memory flashed a clear picture.

* * * * *

HE had fallen asleep over his *Relations of Equity to Common Law*, to be awakened late by clear and curious music outside the house. His study and his bedroom leading off it were on the ground floor. His study window lay open to the lawn. He stepped out, walked a few paces, and there at the angle of the building by the curve of the entrance drive stood the musician. He was an ordinary young man in a soft felt hat, and he played a flageolet which gleamed silver in the starlight. Cosmo Paradyne stood bemused and fascinated, for never had he heard such wonder from a flageolet. It was like the song of birds; the song of trees, of streams, of woods; the song of laughter, of dainty frolic, of elfin devilry. Now it broke into trills of a joy so exquisite that he caught his breath; now into phrases of longing that gripped his heart. And it was all based on a motif which he had not heard before, of which he had not dreamed of hearing, simple as the music of the wind, yet subtle as though it harped upon the rays of a star.

The young man ceased suddenly, advanced, took off his hat and held it out for alms.

'I'm glad you don't mind my playing,' said he. 'Many people tum me away. Last night I had a dog set on me, to my extreme discomfort.'

THE YOUNG MAN CEASED SUDDENLY

'But you're a musician. An extraordinary musician,' said Paradyne.

The young man laughed frankly. 'I rather think I am,' said he. And he edged his hat an inch or two nearer.

To bestow upon this amazing minstrel the largess of a shilling were impossible. He fumbled in his case and dropped a pound note into the hat.

I thank you, sir, for your bounty, ' said the young man, pocketing the note. He put on his hat with a flourish and prepared to turn.

'Excuse me,' said Paradyne, 'I happen to be an amateur clarinettist, and I thought I knew as much as any man living of the music written for wind-instruments; but the thing you were playing just now I can't recognize.'

I 'm sure you can't,' replied the young man pleasantly. 'It is my own composition, and it has never even been set down on paper; much less published for amateurs saving your presence-to make a hash of. Again, sir a million thanks. Good night.'

He swept a bow and marched off. Paradyne went into the house, with the music ringing through his brain.

The next morning to chambers. It was all perfectly clear. Griffiths had brought his elderly client, Miss Phillibert, to consultation.

Wait a bit. He sat on the caravan steps again. Something rather funny had happened. Yes. In the middle of it he had started to whistle and had been brought back to his senses only by the staggered expression on the faces of solicitor and client. He had been whistling this damned tune.

* * * * *

HE lunched at his club, at a solitary table, not feeling equal to jaunty companionship. Then home to Ealing where, feeling ill and jaded, he went to bed. There, in spite of his wife's protests, did he remain. Martha did not believe in people staying in bed unless they came out in spots or betrayed malaise by other unmistakable physical symptoms. It upset the routine of the house. Still, he was the master. She would give the necessary orders. For dinner he had a sole which Martha called fried, but which he, with elementary humour, called dried; whereupon she went off, taking leave of him with acerb courtesy.

Later, servants came to make his bed and see to the comfort of his night. He rose, put on his dressing-gown, and felt very much the better for his rest. He bade the butler set out his golfing things in readiness for the morrow Sunday. He went into his study next door. Being at a loose end, for to-night no work was possible, he bethought him of

Tuesday's early start for Boulogne. Better get everything in readiness now, there being no principles in life more imperative than foresight and method. So, idly, he got together, from the mentally docketed and locked drawers in which they lay, his bundle of ten-pound notes, his store of French money left over from last year's golfing holiday, his yellow Cook's tickets procured a few days ago with their reservations of Pullman and Private Cabin, his letter from the Le Touquet hotel confirming his order for rooms, a little wad of visiting cards, a prescription for a tonic and another for indigestion pills and a very dirty card setting forth, in tabulated form, the mathematical rules for the banker's draw at Chemin de Fer. Having passed the lot in review he stuffed them into his special leather holiday wallet, which, entering his now prepared bedroom, he laid upon the dressing table, intending to lock it up in the drawer.

Now, did he, or didn't he? He couldn't remember.

At any rate, what was certain was that, when he re-entered his study to turn out the light preparatory to going to bed, he heard the infernal young man in the garden playing his fantastically diabolical tune. Again he went forth-this time in pyjamas and dressing-gown—and again he stood entranced till the musician ended and came forward smiling, with outstretched hat.

'Go on, go on,' cried Paradyne.

'Alas, I have but one piece,' said the young man, 'and I only play it once.'

Paradyne flapped his hands against empty night pockets.

'I'm sorry—' he began.

'Don't mention it.'

'I must go into the house, and—'

'I pray you, don't.'

'Will you come to-morrow night?'

The young man cocked his head at a humorous angle and smiled, holding up a protesting hand. 'I only came to-night because you seemed to appreciate my music. But to-morrow—? Do you think I'm going to spend my life in Ealing?'

The very words of his daughter, Viola. He put his hands up to his temples as though to steady an odd rocking.

He said:

'Who are you? Tell me. I should very much like to know.'
'Ah, that's my secret,' laughed the young man.

And mockingly he put the flageolet to his lips and played a few bars, the *motif* of his melody.

'Wait, please,' cried Paradyne. 'You interest me enormously. I can't let you go without—I shan't be a moment.'

He turned the corner, crossed the lawn, and entered the house through the French window of the study. When he returned, Treasury note in hand, the musician had dis appeared. He opened the wooden gate of the circular entrance drive and looked up and down the road in vain search for the musician.

Sleep was impossible. It was a hot night in early June.

Through his brain rang the tantalizing music. He rose. 'I'm going crazy,' said he. 'I must walk it off.'

Never had he done such a thing in his decorous life as to get out of bed and take a midnight walk. But now he did it. He clad himself in his golfing things, laid ready to his hand, and going through his study, locking the door behind him and putting the key in his pocket, he marched out. He marched out along the white respectable road bordered by the grounds of respectable villas, swinging his stick, with a feeling of schoolboy freedom. And, suddenly, in the distance he heard the abominable tune.

HE MARCHED ON ALONG THE WHITE, RESPECTABLE ROAD

And then? And, then, all was blank. Behind that and his present awakening, blank, nothingness, darkness, what you will.

He argued it out in lawyer-fashion. There was the young man's silver flageolet on the grass. That meant that he must have overtaken him and by some means got possession of the instrument. Possibly he had wandered some distance in his company, and had fainted by the way. He realized that he had been on the verge of a nervous breakdown. What more simple explanation than that, he cracking up altogether, his friend had stuffed him into this gipsy caravan, while he and the owner had gone off to the nearest town for medical assistance? So it was Sunday morning after all, and his walking terror lest he should have missed his Monday application before the Judge was futile.

'Splendid,' said he, 'splendid!' He rose and thrust his hands into the pockets of his Norfolk jacket. In the left hand pocket he felt the key of his study window. He laughed aloud and called himself a silly ass.

It was now broad daylight. a wooden gate a few yards ahead of him opened, and a small girl in a blue smock emerged, holding in her hand a bottle of milk. She came towards him and piped childishly:

'*Voici le lait, Monsieur.*'

'What?'

It was a roar of bewilderment at which the child shrank back, frightened.

'*C'est le lait que Monsieur a commande, hier soir.*'

My God,' said he.

'*C'est six sous, Monsieur,*' said the child, holding out her hand.

He was in France after all. Of that he now had no need to be assured by the child's speech and attire. a glance around the infinite plain, dotted sparsely with red-roofed farm buildings and crossed by dead straight line of poplars marking roads like the one in front of him gave him full evidence. But how he had got to France, what he was doing there with a hawker's caravan and a horse, he had no notion. And whereabouts in France was he? Certainly not near Le Touquet.

'Where does this road lead to?' he asked, waving a hand. 'Why Chartres, Monsieur. Ten kilometres. Are you not going to the fair?'

She touched a chord that awakened echoes of dreamland. His sub-conscious self had already registered a long while ago, it seemed, the fact of the fair at Chartres. The child still held out her hand and murmured her claim for six sous. a plunge into his trousers pocket brought up a handful of French money. He gave her a franc and waved her away. She ran off somewhat scared by his madness, but exuberant at his generosity.

"WHY CHARTRES, MONSIEUR, TEN KILOMETRES?"

'I give it up,' said Cosmo Paradyne.

But he didn't. In the breast-pocket of his golfing jacket he found the traveling wallet which he had filled that Saturday night at Ealing. He examined its contents. One first-class ticket for London to Boulogne-that was obviously the one destined for Martha; his own he must have used; three ten-pound notes-he had put ten into the wallet; so he must have changed seventy pounds English money. a wad of French hundred-franc notes. Cards and prescriptions. The soiled Chemin de Fer card. Also a new document or two. One, a dirty piece of coarse paper which he unfolded, was a receipt in French, villainously written and spelled, for the purchase of the caravan, stock and horse. It was made out in his name, Monsieur Cosmo Paradyne. It was duly stamped, signed Galeo Gaspard, and dated the twelfth of June. He scratched a puzzled head. That was Tuesday in Whitsun week. The dates in his mind were clear. The Courts rose on the eighth. He had decided to start for Le Touquet on the fifth. The night when he went forth from his house, key in pocket, was that of Saturday the second of June. Ten days therefore had elapsed between his midnight walk and his purchase of this ridiculous outfit.

Another document, stamped with the stamp of the Republic, was a hawker's licence.

He sighed and entered the caravan, hung, roof and sides, with pots and pans and gaudy scarves and encumbered with battered cases of cheap cutlery, and perceived at the end a cupboard, which, when opened, he found to be stored with food and cooking utensils. There was half a vast circular loaf; eggs, butter, coffee, a good twelve inches of mighty sausage. On the floor stood a tin ewer filled with water. He found also an elementary toilet equipment which, certainly, had never seen Ealing.

For Cosmo Paradyne the history of the next hour or two was surprise piled on astonishment. a glimpse in a small hanging mirror showed a bronzed almost youthful face and clear eyes. His hands were brown and the palms curiously hardened. To make coffee and boil eggs for the satisfaction of an unprecedented hunger seemed a matter of everyday habit. He ate the food with extraordinary relish. As he shaved and washed, there lurked at the back of his mind a dim consciousness of having gone through the same performances amid the same surroundings for a long time past. He seemed to know that stuffed away at the bottom of the cupboard were his golf stockings and knickerbockers and cap. a prescient glance around showed him on a ledge a coarse, peasant's straw hat with a floppy brim which he recognized as his ordinary daily wear. He put it on and went out into the early morning sunshine and drew great breaths of the sweet air.

He laughed, exhilarated by a new sensation as though he had undergone a radical physical change. What was it? It took him some time to realize that never before had he been conscious of such supreme and exhilarating health. It was a joy to feel the spring in his mere tread. He lit his pipe and hands in pockets stared, with proprietary air, over the illimitable landscape of La Beauce. Then he walked round his perambulating property. a big-boned brown horse ceased his munching as he approached and thrust forth a questing muzzle. At the back of the vehicle he found a bag of provender and a wooden pail of water from which he administered to the animal's needs.

He reflected for a moment. There was a horse, there was a thing on wheels. The logical procedure was to harness the horse and travel on, all the more because no earthly purpose could be served by remaining stationary in the wilderness.

It was only when he had attached the animal, in the most business-like way, between the shafts, that he began to wonder how the deuce he had managed to do it. His life had been passed remote from horses. Never had he driven or ridden, still less, harnessed one. It was amazing.

Stooping down he picked up the silver flageolet which he had all but forgotten. How went the air which he had played that morning and which had brought back those clear pictures of his garden in Ealing? He could not remember. Even with the instrument to his lips and his fingers on the stops he could not recall it. It had gone like elfin music heard in a dream.

'Its all damned queer,' said he.

For a while past there had been a scant traffic along the endless road; farmers' carts, lumbering waggons and here and there a brisk little ramshackle motor-car. He clambered to the platform above the shafts, took the reins and the horse moved on at a sober walk. He lit another pipe and reconstructed his elusive history. And now, having got his brain into working order, he concentrated it on the facts such as he knew them. The key in his pocket, the singularly unclean shirt that he was wearing, proved that he had journeyed straight from Ealing to his p resent position near Chartres. He had therefore mysteriously disappeared from his home. He grasped at the sudden realization of what this must have meant to Martha.

He dropped the reins and sat, feet dangling, horror stricken, while the horse plodded stolidly on. For the twenty years of their married life, during his brief and rare absences from home, she had never been without full news of his whereabouts. She must have been, must still be, frantic with anxiety. He must telegraph to her at once. Why not leave this ridiculous gipsy van on the road and beg a lift from the first passing car to Chartres? Possibly, if one had passed just then, he would have obeyed the impulse. But these were days long before the war, when small busy cars were not yet as ants along the roads of France.

HE LIT ANOTHER PIPE

By the time one rattled by, his exact mind had grappled with the circumstances. That he should be the hero of a 'mysterious disappearance' was incredible. Martha, a capable woman, would at once have put the police on his track. a well-known man dressed in golf clothes and without any luggage couldn't make his way from London to Folkestone to Boulogne, without leaving behind him a thousand traces of his passing. People didn't disappear in such simple and casual fashion. The sensitive network of civilization rendered it an impossibility. If he had been wandering about suffering from loss of memory, some tactful messenger would have discovered him and brought him home.

THE HORSE, WITHOUT HIS CONSCIOUS GUIDANCE, TOOK THE BEWILDERED MAN TO CHARTRES

Well, he would send his telegram, give the caravan to the first blind beggar, and start at once for England. How he should manage to account for his defection in the matter of 'Phillibert v. Phillibert, Cohen & Smith,' he did not know. But he surely could get back in time for the re-opening of the Courts-the Trinity sittings-and leave the necessary excuses to the wit of his excellent clerk. He had a heavy couple of months before him. The old sixteen hours a day grind. Loss of memory or not, he must have had a marvellous holiday to put him in t his pink of physical condition.

'Poor old Mart ha must know,' said he.

He found himself all at once in a low, whitewashed village straggling on each side of the road. Outside an estaminet decorated with the double dice box indicating that it was also a *débit de tabac* hung a row of newspapers in a tin file. It struck him that he had not seen a paper for some days. He descended and bought one.

It bore the date of the tenth of September.

* * * * *

THE horse, without his conscious guidance, took the bewildered man to Chartres. There he pulled new-found wits together. He took his midday meal in the *salle à manger* of a humble inn full of country folk who had come for the morrow's fair. His caravan he had left by the wayside on the entrance avenue of plane-trees, in charge of a shock headed boy, one of a family owning a yellow-and-red-striped caravan, apparently in an analogous line of business with his own. In those far-off blissful days, a five-franc piece shone vast and silvery before lowly eye s.... He had entered the humble inn instinctively, as one accustomed to such accommodation, without giving a thought to the pretentious Hôtel du Grand Monarque on the great *place*, where the refined of all nations naturally sought their sustenance.

He sat down at a crowded table between a wizened, blue-bloused peasant with a cropped white head and a neck like that of a moulting parrot craning over a dingy white collar around which was tied a half-inch of black ribbon by way of cravat, and a buxom farm-wife in spotless head-gear,brilliant silk neckerchief and great gold earrings. They ate lusciously with great clatter and prestidigitation of knives, and drank the little grey stony wine, and talked of crops and cattle and marriages and deaths.

And Paradyne, as brown and dusty and with as little outer pretensions to gentility as any of them, found himself talking to his neighbours of these elemental things with a familiarity born of custom. And then from the lady: 'Monsieur was a stranger in the *pays?*' Yes, he was a *marchand forain*, a hawker. He sold a bit of everything and went where he thought the market was best. She opined that one must make *pas mal*-a tidy bit-of money. But for herself she did not like the adventurous life. Not that she had tried it. She could not conceive happiness outside the family. *Tiens*, she had a husband-she made a movement of her head towards a food-absorbing male by her side-and five children. She lived at Gallardon eighteen kilometres off, and had no desire to travel. Once had she been to Paris; but *oh, la, la!* No, truly the family was the only thing. But he must have a family somewhere?

Like Peter he denied instantly. No, he was alone, taking his food where he could find it. In her Gaulish fashion she twitted him with having families scattered along the high roads of France. This delicate impeachment he again denied, whereupon the lady, with a laughing glance out of dark eyes, and an '*allons donc!*' thrust an arch elbow into his ribs. And when her husband claimed her attention, he talked to the old farmer about weather and wheat and apples and *rillettes*, the sausages that were served to them, and all the other wonders of La Beauce. And Cosmo Paradyne knew that for three months he had been leading this life of open air and earth and primitive interests, and, in some odd way, had fallen victim to its fascination.

"TIENS, SHE HAD A HUSBAND"

On a hurried, worried holiday some years before he had visited Chartres with his wife, and had made his intellectual man's pilgrimage to the cathedral.

Be it insisted on here, by the way, that no haggis was more tightly stuffed with giblets and oatmeal than was Cosmo Paradyne with knowledge. From pre-Winchester days onwards he had been the paragon of examinees. His career had been one of meteoric brilliance. In his course he had made himself easy master of three foreign languages, German, Italian and French; his musical ear, his one esthetic gift, had caught and assimilated the accents; after a day or two among a foreign peasantry he could reproduce their intonations, and his marvellous memory could store the patois words which he picked up.... So was he master of the historical or archeological side of the arts of painting and architecture. His mind had ever been receptive of facts, and, tenaciously holding them, of coordinating them into an imperishable crystallization. With such mental qualities, is it to be wondered at that, at forty-two, he was one of the leaders of the Chancery Bar? 'What a judge the little devil will make when he's sick of making money!' said his brethren. On his previous visit therefore to the Cathedral of Chartres, Cosmo Paradyne, drawing from the vast stores of his learning, gave his wife an accurate account of the history of the fabric. He showed her that portion which dated from the middle of the thirteenth century, the stained glass of the same period, the Renaissance screen, the difference between the one twelfth-century spire and the other of the sixteenth century. The Cathedral was, to him, an agglomeration of fascinating facts. Martha had listened distractedly and eventually had replied:

'Yes. That 's very interesting; but I think it 's rather pretty, all the same.'

Having nothing to do, he strolled through the rising ground from which the stupendous edifice commands the plain whose horizon is as vast as that of mid-ocean. Suddenly the tricksy memory that had been playing the devil with him of late captured, unsummoned, the air of the silver flageolet. He hummed it, and somewhat impatiently dismissed it from his thoughts, as he entered the wonder of heaven-seeking piers and shafts of vast spaces and of stained colours of glass through which the sun of the September afternoon streamed ineffably.

He sat on a rush-bottomed chair near the font and drank the glory in like a man parched by a lifelong thirst. He went out very tired, hanging his head, feeling half-drunken. He sat on the low parapet of the parvis and remembered words of long ago flitted through his brain: 'You see that masonry-restored after the fire—' and so on, and so on; and Martha's acid voice: 'Rather pretty, all the same.'

He spread out his hands drunkenly and rushed into the cathedral again and gave himself up to the immensity of its loveliness.

Later he called at the Post Office seeking the answer to a long, explanatory telegram which he had sent to Martha from the village where he had learned the date. He must obtain news of her before starting on his homeward journey. In the cathedral he had been so happy; drenched in a sensuous envelopment of beauty. In the crude hall of the Post Office, before the wire-surrounded pigeon-hole, existence shrivelled into sordidness.

As a piece of identification he handed his hawker's licence through the aperture and waited, while search was made, with a grim smile on his face. Cosmo Paradyne, K.C., was developing a sense of humour a scrubby official in a dirty brown holland smock handed him a gummed-up bit of blue paper.

He read:

'In view previous telegrams cannot believe loss of memory story. Conduct disgraceful. Have kept up fiction of nervous breakdown and foreign holiday for the family's sake. To avoid scandal am willing to receive you. Wire date arrival so that I can announce beforehand. Martha.'

He reeled out of the Post Office. What were the telegrams to which she alluded?

* * * * *

HOWEVER, his deduction had been exact. Martha had known where he was. There had been no mysterious disappearance to make a newspaper sensation. All that was to the good. Martha had also saved his face. Doubtless, the excellent Gregson had returned his briefs with satisfactory explanations. He could go back and take up his work in the most natural way in the world. He could go back and take up Martha who was 'willing to receive ' him.

He noted that the telegram bore the place name Padding ton. It was characteristic of Martha not to trust to the Ealing Post Office, but to take the train in order to send the message from the London Terminus.

Martha was not sympathetic. Obviously she distrusted him; and, her mind being on the track of an imaginary paramour, she would add a rasp to a life that only mutual indifference had kept smooth. Well, he certainly had suffered some mental disturbance, and, if he had followed anybody it was not a woman, but must have been the easy young man with the silver flageolet. But Martha would never believe it, even though he showed her the instrument and played the bewitching tune.

It was dusk when he reached his caravan by the wayside of the plane-tree avenue. His neighbours courteously informed him of their jealous care of his possessions. They had watered and fed the horse, and had guarded the vehicle as though it had been the Ark of the Covenant. Paradyne again bestowed largess on the shock-headed boy. The family sprawled on the grass eating their evening meal. The sight reminded him of his own healthy hunger. He unlocked his door and produced his rough store of food, the main part of which was his sturdy twelve inches of sausage and a bottle of red wine which he discovered with two others, wrapped up for safety's sake in his golfing knickerbockers. He sat on the steps and ate his supper with an enjoyment that, in his memory, had never attended physical things. He had despised the men who wasted their time and talk on flavours of food and wine. He could not tell old port from new, nor had it mattered to him whether he drank it with walnuts or with mackerel. But that evening a great truth dawned on him. The salty, pungent, garlicky sausage and the new coarse wine were predestined for each other in Heaven's Buttery. He ate and drank with an almost palpitating joy.

He filled his pipe with cheap French tobacco and the first puff or two fell into harmony with the wine and the sausage. Its perfume mingled with that of dust and beasts and the warm September smell that arose in the gathering night from the near city and the vast, environing plain. 'My God,' said he, 'it's good to be alive.'

And as he said it, his memory flashed back to the inexplicable words of Martha on the night of Viola's wedding:(—it isn't funny looking after a dead man.'

'What the devil did she mean by that? ' he had asked himself.

Now came a glimmering of the answer in the form of another question: was he so sure that then, and, indeed, all his life before, he hadn't been a dead man?

The phrase worried him for a while. He had a dim, uneasy feeling that he had used it, as Viola's and the young man's remark about Ealing, in the forgotten telegrams. Well, well. He shrugged his shoulders. What did it matter? In a day or two he must inevitably learn their purport. Sufficient for the night was the beauty thereof. A damned queer thing, beauty. He mused. He had known it, of course, as an intellectual conception. But now, it was an emotional matter. It plucked at things within his inmost being and swept unimagined chords. The Cathedral. This dreamy fruitful plain, panting for the soon-coming swell of moonlight.

Yes, he must go back. But things would never be quite the same.

The friendly neighbours in the red-and-yellow-striped caravan busied themselves with preparations for departure. They must take up early position in the fair-ground, according to police regulations. They advised Monsieur to do the same. Monsieur, smoking contentedly, replied that he had plenty of time before him, and watched them start. They made polite farewells.

The last to do so was the obvious sister of the shock headed boy, a half-gipsy wench in the early twenties, artlessly clad in soiled and scanty raiment, but superb in the flowing contours of her lithe youth, and in her coarse loveliness.

'A demain, Monsieur.'

'A demain et bonsoir, Mademoiselle,' said he with a smile and a bow.

She lingered a few instants holding him with eyes half mocking, half-alluring. Then, with an ironical toss of her head, she turned and faded into the dusk. Only when she had gone, did he realize that, during his meal, his gaze had rested pleasurably and conjecturingly upon her; and now her startling picture was imprinted on his mind. She was but a slatternly wild thing, unwashed, unkempt; the only external note of the picturesque about her being a flaming orange neckerchief; living on the fringe of civilization, with possibly no morals to speak of. But, God! She was alive!

* * * * *

FOR the first time in his cramped existence, he grew vehemently aware of the wonder of woman as magnificent woman, of her wonder as elemental complement of man. It had been only the flash of a dark-eyed drab across his vision. But the flash awakened him, so that he gasped, to the mighty potentialities of life. God! That girl was alive in all her sensuous and animal mystery. And he-he smote his brow-he, too, was alive. Lustily alive.... The thought stole into his brain: Martha-Martha who had twitted him with being a dead man-had she ever been anything else but a dead woman? What of the physical mystery of the flesh, which this girl of naught had suddenly pro claimed, had he ever dreamed of conjecturing from the cold and acid woman whose lips conventionally kissed had been as unresponsive as the hem of her garment? Nothing. As woman, newly revealed, Martha was dead. And she loved her living death, gloried in it, strove to maintain all who came near her within the sphere of its blight.

His ears heard the roar, and his eyes beheld the welter of the vast waters of strange emotions and fierce passions and intolerable joys that had ever beaten against the arid fortress in which he had been content to have his bleak and indifferent being.

He wiped the sweat from his brow and leaned dejected against the jamb of the caravan door. What a mighty and dreadful power was Fate. No wonder the Greeks made their gods bow down before its supremacy. The irony of it. Again a Greek conception. The Greeks were right. How otherwise could he explain the staggering situation in which he found himself? What but the relentless cruelty of Fate compelled him, at that moment when the world revealed itself in terms of vital beauty and infinite meaning, to return as return he must, to the old withered life of Ealing and the blight of Martha, and the routine of brain-exhausting, nerve-atrophying, soul-killing, meaningless drudgery in the Court of Chancery? What single hour's happiness had he, intellectual automaton, ever got out of it? What had his brain-cramped life held that could compare with that morning's thrill of intense physical fitness, with that evening's leap towards the Unknown of Passion?

'Oh, damn!'he said despondently.

According to his duty as husband and man of grave responsibilities, he ought even now to be on his way to Paris. But he had been too weary of spirit to make the effort; at any rate too much in love with the day's strange freedom. Besides, how could he leave caravan and horse adrift? The caravan he might have abandoned. Its value was of no account to a man of his fortune. But the horse was a living thing, a creature of responsive sentiment, like a dog. It rubbed its muzzle against his arm as though to manifest fondness. He must make fair and square provision for the horse. To-night's friendly encounter had showed him the way. To-morrow, at the fair, would he sell for a song the whole outfit to his late kindly neighbours; and then the stern and relentless journey back to England.

The gradual traffic going fair-wards passed him by. But he did not hear it, wrapped in his despairing thoughts. The night wore on. The full moon arose, and, shining through the over-arching vault of foliage, fantastically diapered the white road.

* * * * *

FROM his breast pocket, at last, he drew the silver flageolet and looked at it in wistful perplexity. He put it to his lips, at first idly and then with a quivering sense of mastery. And lo! he played the whole of the melody through from beginning to end with its song of birds and its elfin laughter and its longings and haunting mockery just as the young man had played it in the starlight of his garden. And, as he played, his heart was uplifted in a strange exultation, such as-he now remembered dimly-had inspired him once before when he had put the flageolet to his lips. He caught at an elusive memory and gripped it hard, and stared wide eyed before him with open mouth.

A bit of waste land by the roadside under the starlight. It looked like a brick-field. They sat on some scattered rubbish. He could just see the young man's clear-cut, humorous face. 'Sir, for my music I'll take what you like to give me. But my flageolet no money can buy. On the other hand, to him who can play my composition through without fault, I yield it gladly.'

Yes; he had played it through from beginning to end. The young man bowed:

'It is yours,' said he....

'But what will you do without it?'

'I have a new tune in my head more suited to the piccolo which I carry in my pocket, and which, indeed, I prefer as an instrument.'

'This,' laughed Paradyne, fingering the silver keys and stops, 'is good enough for me.'

'Perhaps for the present. But you will grow more fastidious. It has none of the woodland softness. The shepherds of Theocritus, if you remember, piped not into metal but into reed that sprang from organic life.'

He pulled out the homeliest little piccolo in the world. Paradyne stretched out a hand. The young man laughed. 'Not yet,' said he. Then suddenly: 'Where are you going?'

'For a walk.'

'So am I. First through France. Then through Italy, then Sicily.'

THE PLAIN, WHOSE HORIZON IS AS VAST AS THAT OF MID-OCEAN

'France, Italy,Sicily—' the faint echo of his murmured response floated back. 'Fortunate young man!'

' Why should you be less fortunate than I? The road is open. Come with me,' said the young man, and laid a hand upon his arm.

Then, as always, the rift in the curtain that veiled the past three months closed suddenly. But the vision, as far as it went, had been startlingly complete.

He laughed aloud as he gazed on the shimmering pipe, and his laughter was informed with the thrill of pride. It had come to him not as a thing chaffered for and sordidly purchased; but as a minstrel's prize, such as, in the times of which Theocritus sang, he might have been awarded by a challenging god.

France. Italy. Sicily. Theocrih Persephone—' How did Wilde's Villanelle go?

'Slim Lacon keeps a goat for thee,
For thee the jocund shepherds wait;
O Singer of Persephone!
Dost thou remember S icily?'

He repeated the final quatrain two or three times, enjoying its flavour. Then, suddenly, inspired with new strength and purpose, he jumped to the ground, harnessed the horse to the caravan, and started down the moonlit avenue to the town of Chartres. But he did not stay at the fair-ground. He passed through and, casting a humorous glance at the yellow-and-red-striped caravan in which the vivid girl lay presumably asleep, blew a kiss to her with his fingers, as to a symbol, and made his slow progress through the narrow streets of the sleeping city.

The dawn found him, with the shining eyes of one awakened to Life's promise, jogging southward on an irrevocable way, never, in this life, to retrace his steps.

Jogging southward on an irrevocable way, never, in this life to retrace his steps.

N
W
E
S

CPSIA information can be obtained
at www.ICGtesting.com
Printed in the USA
LVHW091634050820
662468LV00001B/391

9 781661 531324